CLEVER
Forgives a Friend

Bob Hartman
Illustrated by Steve Brown

DAVID C COOK®

transforming lives together

CLEVER CUB FORGIVES A FRIEND
Published by David C Cook
4050 Lee Vance Drive
Colorado Springs, CO 80918 U.S.A.

Integrity Music Limited, a Division of David C Cook
Brighton, East Sussex BN1 2RE, England

The graphic circle C logo is a registered trademark of David C Cook.

All Scripture paraphrases are based on the ESV® Bible (The Holy Bible, English
Standard Version®), copyright © 2001 by Crossway, a publishing ministry of
Good News Publishers. Used by permission. All rights reserved.

Library of Congress Control Number 2022946449
ISBN 978-0-8307-8470-7
eISBN 978-0-8307-8639-8

© 2023 Bob Hartman
Illustrations by Steve Brown. Copyright © 2023 David C Cook

The Team: Laura Derico, Stephanie Bennett, Judy Gillispie, James Hershberger, Susan Murdock
Cover Design: James Hershberger
Cover Art: Steve Brown

Printed in China
First Edition 2023

1 2 3 4 5 6 7 8 9 10

012723

One cloudy morning, Clever Cub sat **SULKING** in a dark corner. And Fred was not there.

Papa Bear could see his cub's **GLUM** face. "Where is Fred?" he asked.

Clever Cub grunted and crossed his arms. "I do not know. And I do NOT care!"

"But you and Fred the bunny are best friends!" Papa Bear was surprised.

4

"*Were* best friends," Clever Cub growled. "That was before he called me a big, **BOSSY** bear-head!"

"Why did he say *that*?" Papa Bear asked.

"For no good reason," Clever Cub muttered. "He wanted to dig up wild carrots. But I *hate* wild carrots. So I said no. Then he got **GRUMPY**!"

5

"I see." Papa Bear nodded. "Friends do **GRUMP** and **GROWL** sometimes. But that's what forgiveness is for."

Clever Cub grunted again. "Well, I am *not* forgiving a carrot-chomping name-caller like Fred!"

"Hmm," Papa Bear said. "Would you like to hear a Bible story?"

"Does it have bunnies or carrots in it?" Clever Cub asked, munching on berries.

"No bunnies!" Papa Bear promised. "And no carrots either. But there are some grumpy people in it."

Papa Bear sat down in the sun. "This story is about a young man named Joseph, who had many brothers. Joseph's father, Jacob, made a beautiful, colorful **COAT** for him. But Jacob didn't make special coats for any of Joseph's brothers. What do you think about that?"

Clever Cub scratched his nose. He always did that when he was thinking. "I think his brothers probably wanted that coat!"

9

"You are right, Clever Cub," Papa Bear said. "They worked hard in the fields tending the flocks. They wanted special gifts from their father too. They became **ANGRY** and jealous. But something made them even *more* angry."

"What happened?" Clever Cub asked.

"Joseph told his brothers about a **DREAM** he had," Papa Bear said. "In his dream, he ruled over his whole family."

"Uh-oh!" Clever Cub shouted. "I guess they did not like those dreams! Did they call Joseph a big, **BOSSY** brother-head?"

"No," Papa Bear said. "But they did call him a **DREAMER**. Then they did something *much* worse!"

"What?" Clever Cub asked.

13

Papa Bear said, "The brothers **PLOTTED** to get rid of Joseph. One day out in the fields, the brothers grabbed Joseph, tore off his coat, and **DROPPED** him into a pit!"

Clever Cub's eyes grew big. "What?!"

Papa Bear looked sad. "It's true! Then the brothers sold Joseph as a slave to some traveling men. When the brothers went home, they made their father think that young Joseph was eaten by a wild animal."

Clever Cub's eyes grew even bigger. "Wha-a-a-t? That is **AWFUL**!"

"Yes, it was," Papa Bear agreed. "But God watched over Joseph. He was taken far from home—to the land of **EGYPT**. He worked hard. Then many years later, the ruler of Egypt, called Pharaoh, had two **STRANGE** dreams. He demanded that someone explain them.

"God helped Joseph, the dreamer, explain the dreams to the ruler. Pharaoh was so impressed that he put Joseph in charge of the whole land!"

"What happened to the brothers? Did they ever get in **TROUBLE**?" Clever Cub asked.

"A time came when, for seven long years, no crops grew," Papa Bear said. "Joseph's brothers came to Egypt to get grain that the ruler had saved up. But they didn't know Joseph was in **CHARGE**."

Clever Cub looked grumpy. "Did Joseph tell those mean old brothers to go away?"

"No, he did not." Papa Bear replied. "Joseph knew what forgiveness is for. Forgiveness brings people together. And God is happy when we forgive each other."

Clever Cub's eyes grew as big as they could get. "**WHA-A-AT?** Joseph **FORGAVE** his brothers?! Even after all the awful things they did?"

Papa Bear chuckled. "God helped him do exactly that! And when his brothers realized that this man in charge of **ALL** Egypt was their own brother, they were scared at first. But forgiveness helped bring their family together again."

Clever Cub scratched his nose. He was thinking hard. "So, if I **FORGIVE** Fred, do you think we will be friends again?"

Papa Bear nodded. "Yes, I do. And I think Fred will forgive you for hating carrots too."

"All right, I will forgive him and say I'm sorry too," Clever Cub said.
"And I guess I could try a **TINY** bite of carrot." Then off he went to
find his friend.

For Clever Readers

Clever Cub is a curious little bear who **LOVES** to cuddle up with the Bible and learn about God! Clever Cub gets grumpy when Fred calls him a name. But when he hears the story of Joseph and his brothers (from Genesis 37; 39:20b–23; 41–42; 45), he learns what forgiveness is for.

Has anyone ever called you a name you didn't like? How did that make you feel? Sometimes friends get grumpy with each other and say mean things. But God can help us forgive. Forgiveness helps make everything right again. Is there anyone *you* need to forgive?